CHIMPS DON'T WEAR GLASSES

LAURA NUMEROFF
CHIMPS DON'T WEAR GLASSES

ILLUSTRATED BY JOE MATHIEU

ALADDIN PAPERBACKS

Also by Laura Numeroff and Joe Mathieu:
Dogs Don't Wear Sneakers

First Aladdin Paperbacks edition October 1998

Text copyright © 1995 by Laura Numeroff
Illustrations copyright © 1995 by Joe Mathieu

Aladdin Paperbacks
An imprint of Simon & Schuster
Children's Publishing Division
1230 Avenue of the Americas
New York, NY 10020

Printed and bound in the United States of America

10 9 8 7 6 5 4 3 2 1

The Library of Congress has cataloged the hardcover edition as follows:
Numeroff, Laura Joffe.
Chimps don't wear glasses / by Laura Numeroff ; illustrated by Joe Mathieu.
p. cm.
Sequel to: Dogs don't wear sneakers
Summary: Even though animals don't normally wear glasses, cook, or read,
if you use your imagination you can see them doing these and even more fantastic things.
ISBN 0-689-80150-5
[1. Animals—Fiction.   2. Imagination—Fiction.   3. Stories in rhyme.]   I. Mathieu, Joseph, ill.   II. Title.
PZ8.3.N92Ch   1995   [E]—dc20   94-20320
ISBN 0-689-82030-5 (Aladdin pbk.)

For Paul Taylor…with love

—L. N.

To my dear wife, Melanie

—J. M.

Chimps don't wear glasses

And zebras don't cook

And you won't see a kangaroo reading a book.

Horses don't hang glide,

Giraffes don't drive cars
And you won't see a piglet saving pennies in jars.

Mice don't join Boy Scouts

And llamas don't shop

And hamsters don't clean
with a broom or a mop.

Reindeer don't square dance

And seals don't fly kites

And weasels don't travel to see all the sights.

Pandas don't pole vault

And camels don't sing

And you won't find a chipmunk who'll ever be king.

Tigers don't ice-skate
And wolves don't use mugs

And you won't see a puppet show put on by pugs.

Now just close your eyes and draw with your mind.
You might be surprised at what you will find…

Like yaks in tuxedos

And hippos on boats

And otters who ride in parades full of floats.

Or lions who juggle

And squirrels on stilts

And lizards who know how to sew handmade quilts.

Or ferrets who garden

And turtles who dine.

But tell me what you see. It's your dream—not mine!